P9-CNC-723

DATE DUE

	DATE DUE		

THE CHICAGO PUBLIC LIBRARY

AVALON BRANCH
8148 S. STONY ISLAND AVENUE
CHICAGO, IL 60617

THE CHICAGO PUBLIC LIBRARY

In almost every part of the world, people believed in dragons. Dragons are so much a part of human culture that some people, called dracontologists, study dragon lore today.

The word *dragon* comes from the Greek word *drakon,* meaning "a huge snake with piercing eyesight." Many dracontologists think that belief in dragons was inspired by sightings of large snakes, or serpents. Over time, dragons took on many distinct forms. Dracontologists classify them into five groups.

SERPENT DRAGONS

LEVIATHAN
(LE-VIE-uh-THUHN)
Hebrew Bible

LAMBTON WORM
England

CARTHAGINIAN SERPENT
(KAR-THUH-JIN-EE-AN)
Ancient Rome

Serpent dragons were said to be found in lakes, rivers, and oceans. These creatures had heads like those of reptiles, horns, and long jaws with the sharpest of teeth. They had no wings or legs, just long, slithering, snake-shaped bodies.

SEMIDRAGONS

Because these dragons were simpler in form than classical dragons, dracontologists call them semi-, or partly, dragons. These fierce creatures usually had the body of a serpent and two legs that sported feet with long, sharp talons. Often they had batlike wings.

LINDORM
Europe

WYVERN
(WHY-VERN)
England

CLASSICAL DRAGONS

CLASSICAL MEDIEVAL DRAGON
England

MEDIEVAL means about the Middle Ages, a time between A.D. 500 and 1500.

A MYTH is a traditional story that explains a belief or natural event.

Classical dragons were said to be ferocious, fire-spitting, reptilianlike creatures. In mythology, they were usually the enemies of valiant heroes. These beasts were covered in a scaly armor. They had taloned feet and long, powerful tails that often ended in an arrow-shaped stinger.

SKY DRAGONS

Semidragons that used their wings for flight were called sky dragons. They drifted and soared around the cloud-filled heavens. Some were even capable of flying without wings. Often they were believed to have magic powers or even to be gods.

AMPHIPTERE
(AM-FIH-TEER)
England

CHINESE DRAGON

BASILISK
Ancient Greece

PELUDA
France

COCKATRICE
(KA-kuh-truhs)
England

TARASQUE
(TAR-USK)
France

Neo- means "to take on a new and different form." Neodragons looked somewhat like the other kinds of dragons, but they were made up of various animal parts. These terrifying creatures had many different forms.

In Mesopotamia four thousand years ago, people explained the creation of the earth with a fierce story about a dragon. They said that in the beginning there was only Aspu, the spirit of fresh water and emptiness, and Tiamat, a female dragon. Aspu and Tiamat were mates.

TIAMAT
(TEE-AH-MAT)

MARDUK

One of their children was Marduk, a powerful god. He fought against his mother and the monsters she had created for battle. In the end, Tiamat lost. Her body became the heavens and the earth, and the blood of the slain monsters was shaped into the human race.

Just as we do today, ancient people loved to hear stories about brave and daring heroes. In Greece, the greatest hero was Hercules, a son of Zeus, king of the gods. One of the most exciting stories about Hercules is how he fought the Hydra, a fierce, many-headed dragon with poisonous breath. This Hydra would leave its den to devour everything in its path. Many had tried to kill it, but all had failed.

Hercules was enraged when he learned about the Hydra. Boldly he set out to destroy this terrible creature. As they battled, one by one the many heads of the Hydra fell to the ground. While the beast lay dying, Hercules dipped his arrows into the Hydra's blood, giving these weapons a magical strength for when he fought again.

Dragons were considered very important by the people of ancient China. For thousands of years, the symbol of the imperial throne was a dragon. Some people believed that dragons brought good luck, such as rain for farmers' crops. Other, more fearsome dragons were said to bring death and disease.

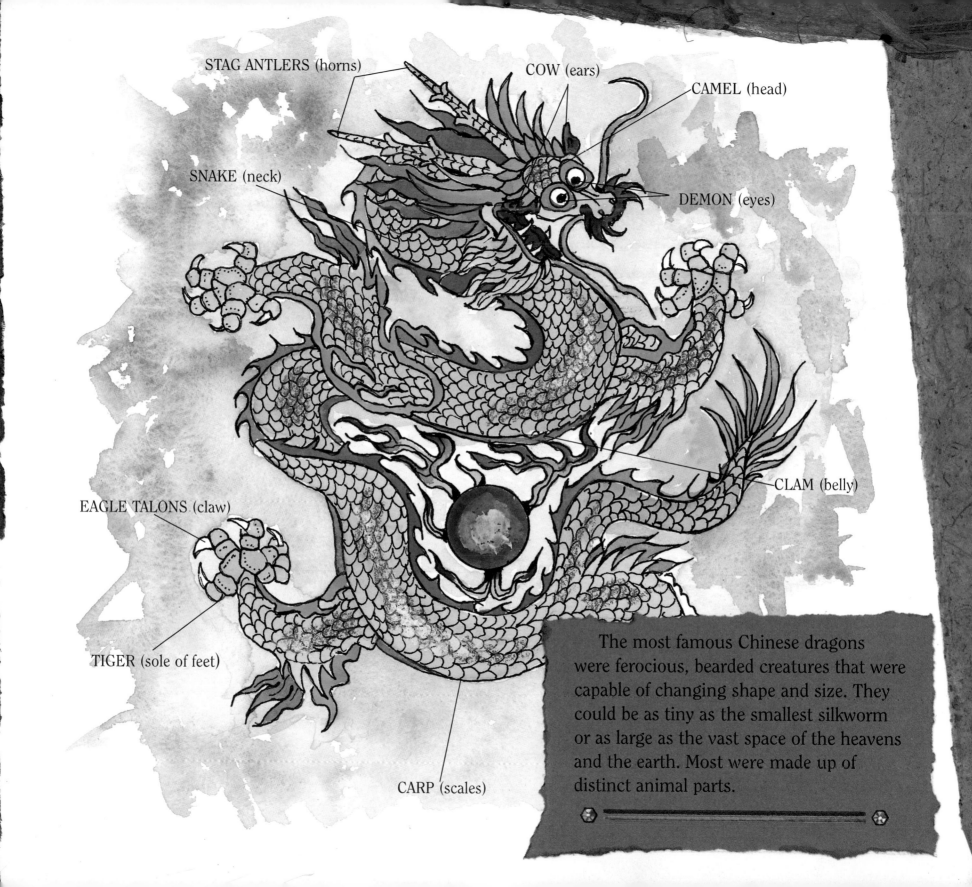

STAG ANTLERS (horns)

COW (ears)

CAMEL (head)

SNAKE (neck)

DEMON (eyes)

CLAM (belly)

EAGLE TALONS (claw)

TIGER (sole of feet)

CARP (scales)

The most famous Chinese dragons were ferocious, bearded creatures that were capable of changing shape and size. They could be as tiny as the smallest silkworm or as large as the vast space of the heavens and the earth. Most were made up of distinct animal parts.

In modern China, the bearded Chinese dragon is still a popular image. During the Chinese New Year parade, celebrants twist through the streets beneath a writhing dragon costume, to keep evil spirits away in the new year.

CELEBRANTS are people who celebrate!

In some religious beliefs, dragons were symbols of evil. Stories portraying great heroes defeating dragons in battle symbolized the war between good and evil, in which good always won.

In eighth-century Northern Europe, people listened to the epic poem about Beowulf (BAY-UH-WULF), the king of a people called the Geats. As a young man, Beowulf killed three terrible monsters. But when he was very old, he had to confront one again—a monstrous treasure-hoarding dragon no one else could defeat.

This fire-spewing dragon swept over Beowulf's domain, destroying farms and villages. Beowulf set out with a small band of warriors to conquer the mighty beast. There was a terrible battle, and at last the dragon was slain. But before it died, it managed to sink its evil fangs in Beowulf's throat. Losing his life slaying a powerful dragon to protect his people—this was a great death for a hero such as Beowulf.

During medieval times, saints were often shown slaying dragons to symbolize Christianity conquering sin. One of the most beloved stories is that of St. George and the dragon. It was said that, long ago, in the North African city of Silene, a rampaging dragon had eaten all the sheep and cattle and now was eating children too! The king was so desperate he decided to sacrifice his own daughter to try to satisfy the terrifying beast.

George vowed to save her. This Roman soldier, now a Christian, released the princess and stood in her place. When the dragon attacked, George quickly put it to death. The people were so grateful that they, too, became Christians. Many centuries later, George was made the patron saint of England for his noble deeds.

Quetzalcoatl (KET-SAHL-CO-AH-TL) was the dragon god of the Aztecs, an ancient people in what is now Mexico. Most of the time, Quetzalcoatl was described as being part serpent and part quetzal, a spectacular feathered bird. He was believed to be the god of wind, wisdom, and life.

In one of the ancient Aztec beliefs, Tezcatlipoca (TEZ-COT-LEE-POCA), the god of trickery and darkness, stole almost all of Quetzalcoatl's magical powers. So Quetzalcoatl sailed away, promising the Aztecs that he'd return more powerful than before. In 1519, when Spaniards arrived in the Gulf of Mexico, the Aztecs welcomed them. Perhaps they believed that Quetzalcoatl had come back at last. Instead, their nation was conquered by the Spanish in two years.

Over time, the dragon has been the symbol of power, strength, and ferociousness. The early Egyptians painted images of dragons to guard and protect their great palaces and pyramids. In medieval times, serpent dragons made from colorful cloth twirled in the wind as they were carried into battle. Dragon images adorned the shields of brave knights.

The stories, myths, and legends of dragons have been woven into tapestries, painted on pottery, formed into jewelry, and carefully painted into books over the ages. What mysterious and changeable beasts they were. Behold…the dragons!

BEHOLD...MORE DRAGONS!

DRACO, THE STAR CONSTELLATION

Greek mythology claimed that during the battle of the Titans, the goddess Athena flung a dragon—Draco—into the sky, where it became trapped among the stars.

UTHER PENDRAGON'S DRAGON

Uther Pendragon, father of the legendary King Arthur, dreamed of a great dragon in the sky. The dragon became a symbol of English might and has been on the battle flag of English kings ever since.

THE GARGOYLE

In medieval France, stories were told of a dragon that spewed torrents of water, flooding and destroying everything in sight. It was called the *gargouille,* or "gargler." When an archbishop threatened it with the sign of the cross, the great beast was extinguished. Because of this connection with a religious figure, the gargoyle turned into a symbol of protection, decorating churches and buildings.

For centuries, people living in Bavaria, Austria, and the Swiss Alps described the tatzelworm as having a catlike head, two clawed feet, and a serpent's body. In 1954, Sicilian farmers claimed a tatzelworm attacked their pigs. Some zoologists are willing to believe that the tatzelworm exists. They think it might be a large undiscovered lizard with a long serpentine body.

Many millions of years ago, the British Isles were home to the prehistoric *Kuehneosaurus,* an elongated lizardlike beast that had wings for soaring through the skies. Today a similar creature still exists in the jungles of Southeast Asia. It is known as *Draco volans,* or "flying dragon."

In Scotland, people have reported seeing a mysterious long-necked animal swimming in the loch, or "lake." No modern-day animal looks like this, but during prehistoric times the plesiosaur looked a lot like the Loch Ness monster, popularly known as Nessie, is described.

The komodo dragon is a giant lizard that was discovered on the Indonesian island of Komodo in 1912. It can grow up to ten feet long and stand up to three feet tall. It feeds mostly on goats, pigs, and deer, but it has been known to eat humans. Its saliva is poisonous and its breath is hideous. This dragon really exists!

THE TATZELWORM

WINGED SERPENTS

THE LOCH NESS MONSTER

THE KOMODO DRAGON

THE CHICAGO PUBLIC LIBRARY